NICK® all grown up!™

Welcome to Fifth Grade!

by Steven Banks

illustrated by Larissa Marantz and Katharine DiPaolo

Simon Spotlight/Nickelodeon

New York   London   Toronto   Sydney

Based on the TV series *Nickelodeon All Grown Up!*™ created by Arlene Klasky, Gabor Csupo, and Paul Germain as seen on Nickelodeon®

SIMON SPOTLIGHT

An imprint of Simon & Schuster Children's Publishing Division
1230 Avenue of the Americas, New York, New York 10020
Manufactured in the United States of America
First Edition 10 9 8 7 6 5 4 3 2 1
ISBN 0-689-86609-7

Tommy Pickles and his best friend, Chuckie Finster, were at Java Lava drinking ice-cold Mega Slurp smoothies.

"Here's to our last day of freedom before school starts!" Tommy said, raising his cup.

Just then Tommy's cousin Angelica walked in.

"Well, if it isn't the big, bad *almost* fifth grader!" she said, smirking at Tommy.

"What's fifth grade like?" he asked anxiously.

Angelica sighed. "That was so long ago, I can hardly remember."

"Don't worry, fifth grade's a piece of cake!" said Chuckie.

Angelica narrowed her eyes. "So, are you worried about the H.T.B.T.S.C.?"

"What's the H.T.B.T.S.C.?" asked Tommy.

Angelica's jaw dropped. "You don't know about the H.T.B.T.S.C.?" She looked around and then whispered, "Meet me in the alley in two minutes!"

As they left to meet Angelica, Chuckie began to worry. "What do you think the H.T.B.T.S.C. is?" he asked.

Tommy shrugged. "There's only one way to find out!"

"Maybe we don't want to find out!" said Chuckie.

Angelica was waiting for Tommy and Chuckie in the alley.

"Okay, you guys," she whispered. "You have to swear that you'll never, ever tell anybody I told you this!"

Tommy and Chuckie raised their right hands. "We swear!"

"H.T.B.T.S.C. stands for the Horrible, Terrible Back-to-School Ceremony!" said Angelica.

"I've never heard of that," said Tommy.

"That's 'cause it's a secret, doofball!" said Angelica. "Every new fifth grader has to go thro this ceremony. If you don't, they won't let you i the fifth grade."

"That's not true!" said Chuckie. "I never ha an H.B.T.S.C.T., and I went to fifth grade."

Angelica rolled her eyes. "It's H.T.B.T.S.C., and you're lucky no one found out that you were overlooked." She paused. "I've got a fabulous idea! I could take you both through the ceremony, and then you'd be done with it!"

"Uh, I don't know . . . ," said Tommy.

"Fine!" said Angelica, walking away. "Let some complete stranger perform the Horrible, Terrible Back-to-School Ceremony!"

"Did *you* go through it, Angelica?" asked Tommy.

"Of course!" said Angelica. "How do you think I got into fifth grade?"

Chuckie grabbed Tommy. "Maybe we'd better do it, Tommy!"

Angelica turned around and smiled. "Meet me at my house at two o'clock."

Angelica was waiting for the boys at her house. "Those lamebrains actually think they have to do this! This is going to be sweet!"

Just then Tommy and Chuckie walked up.

Angelica spoke in a low voice. "Let the Horrible, Terrible Back-to-School Ceremony begin!

"First you have to walk around the block wearing your underwear on your head," she said.

Tommy laughed. "I haven't done that since I was two years old!"

"No way!" Chuckie protested. "I'm out of here!"

"Fine," said Angelica. "Don't say I didn't warn you."

"I can't believe we're actually wearing underwear on our heads in public," said Chuckie.

Tommy grinned. "Maybe we're starting a new fashion trend, and everybody will start doing it."

"I don't think so!" said Chuckie. "Walk faster!"

Angelica then gave them their next task. "Now you have to stand in the middle of the park and sing 'Row, Row, Row Your Boat' ten times in a row . . ."

Tommy shrugged. "That doesn't sound too tough."

". . . wearing flowers in your hair!" said Angelica.

"Row, row, row your boat, gently down the stream . . . ," sang Tommy and Chuckie.

Angelica was laughing hysterically until people started putting money in Chuckie's hat!

"All right!" shouted Tommy. "We're making money!"

"They like us!" said Chuckie. "They really like us!"

Angelica made Tommy and Chuckie do all sorts of crazy things. By the end of the day, they were exhausted.

"Are we done yet, Angelica?" pleaded Chuckie.

Angelica shook her head. "There's just one more thing before the ceremony's over."

"Bring it on!" said Tommy.

Angelica grinned. "You have to dress up as girls and go into Java Lava and order Mega Squeeze juices and drink them!"

"No way!" cried Chuckie. "I can't do that! I may want to go into politics someday!"

"Just pretend it's Halloween," said Tommy.

The boys did what Angelica asked. They were about to leave when their friends Lil and Phil walked in!

"Hi, girls," said Phil. "New in town?"

"I'm Lil and this is my brother, Phil," said Lil.

Tommy thought quickly. "Uh, I'm Tammy and this is Charlotte, and we gotta go!"

Phil watched them run out. "Wow! Those were the two ugliest girls I've ever seen!"

"We did it!" shouted Tommy. "Now we're official!"

Angelica was laughing so hard she started crying!

"What's so funny?" asked Chuckie.

"*You* are!" said Angelica, holding her stomach as she roared with laughter. "There is no H.T.B.T.S.C.! I made the whole thing up!"

"That was mean!" said Tommy.

"No, it wasn't!" said Angelica. "It was hysterical!"

"ANGELICA PICKLES!" called a voice.

Angelica turned around to see three older seventh-grade girls.

The tallest one spoke. "Come with us."

"Cool," said Angelica. "Are we going to a party?"

The girl shook her head. "No. It's time for your Really Awful Induction into Seventh Grade!"

"*I've never heard of that!*" Angelica protested.

The girl smiled. "That's because it's a secret!"

Tommy and Chuckie waved as Angelica walked off with the girls.

"Good luck, Angelica!" shouted Chuckie.

Tommy turned to his friend. "So? Ready for school tomorrow, Chuckie?"

Chuckie grinned. "After what we just went through? Piece of cake!"